The Little Red Christmas Ball

A story for kids
and
anyone who ever was...
and
would be again

by
Brian Moloney

ISBN-13: 978-0692678282
ISBN-10: 069267828X

Keymaker Publishing

Email: freelanceretort@gmail.com

Cover Design: Brian Moloney

Christmas Ball image ©CoolCLIPS.com
Background image ©christmasstockimages.com

Also by Brian Moloney

The Kingdom of Keys
(Young Adult Fantasy/Adventure/Fiction)

Available thru all major on-line booksellers

Dedication

To my Mom & Dad (Chris & Bernie) who provided a

warm, safe, happy place that allowed all the Little Red
Christmas Balls rolling around in my head to always shine
bright and hold tight....

The Little Red Christmas Ball
Table of Contents

Part I
"It's Time"

In a faraway corner of a dark dusty attic stood a small stack of time worn old boxes. Inside one of the oldest boxes, nestled in a blanket of aged, yellowed newsprint, the Little Red Christmas Ball yawned awake from a long, peaceful, waiting sleep.

Amid the tales of yesterday he'd waited. Through the soft bloom of spring to the crisp colors of autumn and winter's shortening light, he'd waited and waited...*and dreamed....*

...It was a happy dream of a brisk winter's day, a long time ago. In the dream, the Little Red Christmas Ball is presented as a gift from a very old man to a very young boy.

"Make sure you take good care of this Little Red Christmas Ball," said the old man in his gruff, stale voice. "I've passed many a happy Christmas with this little fellow and he's always taken good care of me. Now, I'm trusting you and I'm passing him on, because...well...because it's time."

"Yes sir," said the little boy, entranced as always by this strange, wrinkled old man. He could almost read the deeply worn lines on his face and he marveled at the wonderful stories they told.

"Yes sir, I promise I'll take real good care of him, sir."

The old man studied the young boy and said, "Yep...yep, I believe you will, I believe you will indeed."

With that he rose and returned to the family festivities, bellowing for his roasted Christmas chestnuts.

It was true; the little boy was fascinated at once by this ordinary, yet exceptionally bright, red little Christmas ball. In its shimmering reflection, the boy could actually see the warmth sparkling in his very own innocent eyes. This made the Little Red Christmas Ball feel very happy and very special...and very lucky to be a Little Red Christmas Ball.

As the years passed, the little boy hung the Little Red Christmas Ball as high on the tree as the little boy could.

And every year, as the little boy grew, the Little Red Christmas Ball rose higher and higher and higher up the tree. As high, it seemed, as a Little Red Christmas Ball could go. But it never really mattered just where he was hung. He knew...he was sure...he thought, that everyone would see. He could shine the brightest because it came from within. And he would be the reddest, the reddest a Little Red Christmas Ball could be....

...Lately, stirring in his slumber, the Little Red Christmas Ball sensed the days were a little bit different from the other endless days. They seemed to sparkle a little bit more. They seemed to tingle a little bit more. They seemed to feel just a little bit...well, just a little bit more. He could smell the magic...yes the magic was in the air. It was his day...it was his time. He knew it was...Christmas time.

Off in the distance he heard the sound of small footsteps running quickly up the stairs. Yes, he was sure...they were here all right. He could hear the laughter. The wonderful sounds of magic and delight. The little ones had arrived—as they did every season—and confirmed, indeed, another had come.

Suddenly, there was the rustle of boxes, hurriedly scooped

up by excited young arms and unceremoniously bumped and brought down the stairs.

The cartons were plopped on soft, sofa cushions and the excitement grew louder as they were jiggled and jounced.

"It's time, it's time, it's time!" cried the Little Red Christmas Ball, happily bouncing up and down...back and forth...side to side.

"Now watch what you're doing. Don't rush, and be careful," said the little boy from the dream, who now was a man with a family of his own. "There's plenty of time and Santa won't come if our tree is a mess."

Now it was the Little Red Christmas Ball who laughed with delight, for he knew that Santa always came, regardless of trees and Little Red Christmas Balls. And while he knew...he thought...he always shone red and he always shone bright, he knew Santa was much too busy to notice any one tree...or a Little Red Christmas Ball.

Quickly and excitedly, the little hands started to pull this and yank that. Paper flew everywhere as one by one a large variety of ornaments lay out before them.

"Don't forget me, don't forget me!" cried the Little Red Christmas Ball, afraid he'd be overlooked in all the commotion. He hadn't missed a Christmas, yet, but with every year passing he seemed to worry more and more he'd be forgotten.

"If a Little Red Christmas Ball missed a Christmas, what would a Little Red Christmas Ball be?"

Over the years, he had seen many old friends come and go. Actually, when he thought about it, he knew he was the last of the bright and colorful breed that had shone brightly from within and lit up the trees of yesterday. In fact, the Little Red Christmas Ball suspected that with each passing season his shine was getting a little less shiny and his special red color a little less colorful. To be perfectly honest, he knew he'd become, well...just a little bit ordinary.

These days, it seemed, all the ornaments had some sort of trick or gimmick they performed. There was that silly Jogging Moose...the obnoxious Dancing Penguins...and those annoying Singing Mice or squirrels...whatever they are.

The Little Red Christmas Ball wouldn't worry about them too much...he thought. None of them had felt the exciting

5

tingle of as many Christmas Eves as he had. They'd never shared the special magic that sparkles and shines in a little one's eyes. Besides, even though, these days, he seemed to spend more time hidden in the back or buried on the bottom, he knew...he thought...there was always plenty of room on the tree for everyone.

"Don't forget me, don't forget me!" shouted the Little Red Christmas Ball.

Abruptly, his wrapper was shed and he was pulled free. At first, the Little Red Christmas Ball was dazzled by the rush of activity surrounding him. The three little children ran excitedly round and round the room as he was cradled in the tiny hands of the littlest boy.

For some reason, he thought, as he softly glowed, *I always seem to attract the littlest ones.*

"Oh, oh... be careful of my hook. If I ever lost my hook I couldn't be hung. Don't drop me, don't drop me," cried the Little Red Christmas Ball to the un-hearing ears of the littlest boy.

Slowly, the familiar surroundings of the warm, cozy room came into focus and the Little Red Christmas Ball began to take inventory.

"There's Grandpa's old rocker...and grandma's favorite wooly comforter...and the fireplace, roaring and filling the room with...smoke...cough, cough...choke cough...and...oh my...how much the children have grown."

There were three of them; two boys and a girl. The Little Red Christmas Ball had been a favorite of them all, at one time or another. But children always seemed to grow up and lose interest in Little Red Christmas Balls. He understood this and came to expect it, too. But he knew as long as he did his job as well as he could...he knew there would always be a place for him in somebody's heart...he hoped...he thought.

"My turn, my turn," shouted the littlest boy. "I will hang this one, I will hang this one!"

This was it. The moment a Little Red Christmas Ball waits for all year. A branch to call his own and a home to cheer.

Now remember, thought the Little Red Christmas Ball, shine bright and hold tight.

"Hey, look over here," shouted the little girl. "It's the Dancing Penguins!"

"Where?" exclaimed the littlest boy, as he ran towards his sister.

"Oh those darn old silly penguins, again," said the Little

Red Christmas Ball. "Don't drop me, don't drop me! Pleeeese be careful!"

"Hey, you guys. I told you to take your time," said the Daddy. "If we try to hang them all at once, we'll end up with a big pile of broken ornaments. Everyone pick your favorites and we'll hang them one at a time."

"Thank goodness for daddies," said the Little Red Christmas Ball. "Now, I see a particularly nice branch way up there in the front...."

"I want the penguins," said the little girl.

"I'll take the moose," said her older brother.

"Not that obnoxious moose," said the Little Red Christmas Ball.

"And I'll take these good ol' Singing Mice or squirrels...whatever they are," said the littlest boy as he absently put a disappointed Little Red Christmas Ball to the side.

So, out of the way, the Little Red Christmas Ball sat and waited...some more. He really didn't mind...he thought. He'd waited a long time and he could wait a little longer...he thought. Besides, from where he was sitting, he could watch all the fun...and he knew there was a nice comfy branch waiting just for him...he hoped.

Up went the Jogging Moose, the Dancing Penguins, the Singing Mice or squirrels...whatever they are, and all the rest. Daddy hung the twinkling lights and the Mommy said, "Leave room for my tinsel. Remember, hang it one strand at a time."

"One strand at a time!" protested the rest.

"I hate dumb ol' tinsel," said the littlest boy as he reluctantly threw clump after clump on the prickly limbs. But he knew, after it was all on the tree, he would love how it sparkled...and besides, Mommy seemed to enjoy putting it on. Are all mommies like that, he wondered?

Quietly, the Little Red Christmas Ball enjoyed all the fuss. After all, it was sort of a privilege to supervise the proceedings.

"You missed a spot there...more to the right...a little higher. No, no, more to the left... lower now lower," directed the Little Red Christmas Ball.

Slowly but surely, the tall skinny evergreen transformed into a sight to behold. The Little Red Christmas Ball had seen it year after marvelous year, yet he'd never gotten over just how beautiful a Christmas tree could be. Every year, it seemed, there was never a tree as magical as the one standing before him.

"Hey, don't forget this Little Red Christmas Ball," said the Daddy. "Why I can remember the day—"

"Quick Daddy, give him to me," said the littlest boy.

"Oh please, don't start telling that old story again," said the Mommy.

"Why, Mommy? I like that Little Red Christmas Ball story," said the little girl.

"Not after you've heard it a zillion times," said the older little boy.

"Oh, alright, alright," said the Daddy as he gently handed the Little Red Christmas Ball to the littlest boy.

"I wouldn't mind hearing that story one more time," said the Little Red Christmas Ball. "It's always been one of my—

Whoooosh!

"Favoriiiiiites...."

In the blink of an eye the Little Red Christmas Ball was swept up and away and sped towards the tree.

"Pick a good spot," said the Mommy.

"Yes, pick a great spot!" said the Little Red Christmas Ball.

Up, up, up...the littlest boy reached, as high as a little boy could...which really wasn't very high at all.

A bit to the side...and more towards the back than he would like...but a branch of his own and a home to cheer.

All that a Little Red Christmas Ball could need.

Finally—he had made it...made it at last.

"Another year, another tree, another Christmas...Hooray!" shouted the Little Red Christmas Ball.

Part II
"Settling In"

As the hours passed, everything was as it should be on Christmas Eve. The family busied themselves, attending to their holiday chores of decorating the house with colorful strands of garland and holly. Mommy hung the mistletoe in her favorite, strategic spot, while the children cautiously stepped around the dreaded plant, laughing at Daddy, who kept walking right under, pretending not to see.

Elsewhere, the Little Red Christmas Ball was busy settling in on his new Christmas home.

"Not a bad little branch," he said, as he cautiously bounced to test his perch. "Firm and steady with plenty of healthy needles. This limb will hold up way past the New Year. Still, it would be a lot nicer if I were just a little bit higher...and more out in front. Oh well, what's a Little Red Christmas Ball to do," he sighed.

Looking around the tree, the Little Red Christmas Ball saw the many familiar faces of recent years, past. He had to admit, they were not without their own particular, although manufactured, holiday charms. Perhaps he'd not really taken the time to get to know them as well as he should have. As he'd said before, there was plenty of room for everyone on the tree. Besides, they're probably a bit in awe of his longevity. Reputations do travel fast on the Christmas tree. Maybe he could share some of his holiday wisdom and experiences. Pass along a few tips, that sort of thing.

"Ah-hem," said the Little Red Christmas Ball, clearing his throat to speak to the Jogging Moose. "In all the time we've been...*hanging out* together," he giggled at his own little pun, "I don't think we've been properly introduced. I am the Little Red Christmas Ball and I've been with this family for more years than I can remember. Perhaps you may have noticed me in the past. Say, that sure is a great spot you've landed in this year."

"What's that you say," puffed the Jogging Moose, as he jogged in place. "I can't hear you too well with these headphones on."

"I said that's quite a nice spot you have this year. Perhaps you may have noticed me in the past," repeated the Little Red Christmas Ball.

"No...can't say as I have," panted the moose. "I've been much too busy with my jogging and all. Can't stop to socialize."

"But where on this tree are you jogging to?" asked the Little Red Christmas Ball.

"Don't know," said the moose. "Just jogging. That's what I do, you know; running and jogging...listening to some cool tunes on my headset."

Toons, toons...what in the Christmas tree are cooltoons? wondered the Little Red Christmas Ball as he turned away from the Jogging Moose.

"Hmmmm, I see the Singing Mice or squirrels...whatever they are...over there across the way; a little bit higher up and more towards the front than I am...naturally," he sighed. "Maybe this would be a good time to find out just what...*exactly*...are they supposed to be.

"Say there," said the Little Red Christmas Ball, full of friendly enthusiasm. "That certainly is a handsome Santa's cap you...uhm...all...are wearing. Perhaps you may have noticed me in the past, I'm—"

"Deck the Halls with boughs of holly..." blared the mice or squirrels...whatever they are...."fa la la la la, la la la.........LA!"

"My goodness!" cried the Little Red Christmas Ball. "You...uhm...fellows...certainly love to sing. I don't suppose you know what a cooltoon is?"

"Fa la la la la, la la la.........LA!"

It was no use, he decided.

"And I won't even consider speaking to those obnoxious penguins. I tried to be sociable, but everyone seems to be all wrapped up in themselves. Much too busy to talk to a Little Red Christmas Ball," he huffed.

As the Daddy and his children approached the tree, the Little Red Christmas Ball's spirits once again rose and his soft glow increased. He noticed they were carrying a bundle of brightly, wrapped gifts.

"Speaking of wrapped up," he exclaimed, "here come some early arriving presents! Oh boy, things are really starting to look like Christmas now! I wonder if it's snowing."

"Be careful now, son," said the Daddy to the littlest boy. "We don't want to knock the whole tree over."

"Don't worry, Daddy, I'm just gonna put Grandpa's present over here."

"No, I was gonna put Grandma's present in that spot," said the little girl, pushing her younger brother out of the way.

"Look out both of you," said the oldest boy, carrying a much too large stack of gifts for aunts, uncles and other assorted relatives.

CRASH....went the stack of presents as the littlest boy pushed his sister...who fell into her older brother...who dropped the gifts...into the tree...and....

"...Ooooooooooh...hooooold tiiiight, everybody," said the Little Red Christmas Ball as the magnificent evergreen rocked wildly back and forth in its little Christmas tree stand. Backward and forward the Jogging Moose swayed. Up and down the Dancing Penguins bounced. Side to side the Singing Mice or squirrels...whatever they are, swung. Around and around the Little Red Christmas Ball spun.

Seconds passed like minutes as the children watched in horror. The Mommy and Daddy held their breath and stood frozen, unable to move, while the tree continued to teeter and totter from side to side.

"Oh no, this can't be happening," cried the Little Red Christmas Ball. "Not now, not after waiting so long."

He'd heard stories of such tragedies. Broken limbs and shattered glass everywhere. Christmas ruined for everyone.

"This couldn't happen, here; not to this family...not to this tree...not to...me...could it? Shine bright and hold tiiiiight!" shouted the Little Red Christmas Ball.

And apparently, the Little Red Christmas Ball was right. For as sure as Santa had a roll-polly belly, the glittering tree slowly came to rest in its former, stately position.

The children exhaled, shrewdly avoiding the needle-like gaze of their parents.

"Now, wouldn't that have been a nice way to spend Christmas Eve?" said the Mommy. "I don't think Santa would have appreciated our beautiful tree in pieces, spread out all over the living room floor."

"He probably would've just turned around with all the

presents and given them to some nice, well-behaved little boys and girls," followed the Daddy.

Now the three little children stopped breathing completely, horrified by that unthinkable thought.

"Oh well," said the Mommy. "I guess there was no real harm done."

"I suppose," said the Daddy. "Besides, it's Christmas Eve and Santa's much too busy to watch over every girl and boy tonight. Let's just hope your record for the year is a good one."

The little girl and oldest boy exhaled a quiet sigh of relief, while the littlest boy wondered, "Just what is considered a good record?"

Up on his now steadied green branch, the Little Red Christmas Ball checked his surroundings for damage.

"Hmmmm, everything and everyone seems to be in place. Thank goodness my hook was secure. Nothing like a little excitement to...*shake-up*...the holiday spirit," giggled the Little Red Christmas Ball.

Part III
"Traditions"

Now, as the last signs of wintry light turned to darkness, the wonder of this special evening returned. The family, again, settled comfortably into their old, familiar traditions. Mommy worked in the kitchen putting the finishing touches on her Christmas Eve dinner. Daddy worked in the garage applying the last coat of paint to a secret surprise. And huddled by the big picture window, three little children worked, searching the stars for signs of snow and other unusual activity.

After the holiday feast was consumed, Daddy did the dishes, while Mommy helped the children climb into pajamas, saved special, just for this night.

"Boy, Mommy, I sure am stuffed," said the littlest boy.

"Me too, I think I might pop like a balloon," said the little girl.

"Not me," said the older little boy. "I think I'll eat that other drumstick, later on...maybe for a midnight snack. Maybe I'll even wait up and make Santa a sandwich when he comes. Yeah...I bet Santa would like that a whole lot better than the cookies and milk we always leave for him. I'll even get him a nice cold beer. Boy won't Santa be extra happy to come here, next year. I bet he'll even leave a few, extra special presents for all of us...even you and Daddy, Mommy," he quickly added.

Whomp...went the pillows as the older little boy was knocked across the room by his brother and sister.

"Stop being silly," said the little girl. "Everyone knows Santa doesn't drink beer. He loves his cookies and milk".

"And don't forget carrots for the reindeers; but not those ol' mushy ones we had for supper...nobody likes those. I mean, probably not reindeers. Right, Mommy?" said the littlest boy, avoiding his mother's harsh stare.

"That's right," said the Mommy, unsuccessfully trying to

hold back a grin. "And I don't think anyone is going to be up at midnight having snacks with Santa. You know he won't come down our chimney until everyone's asleep."

"Make sure Daddy puts the fire out before he goes to bed," said the little girl.

"He will," said the Mommy. "But I think Santa wears fireproof boots."

"But what about his beard, Mommy?" said the littlest boy. "His beard could catch on fire."

"Yes Mommy, please make sure Daddy puts out the fireplace," repeated the little girl.

"Ok, ok, I promise," said the Mommy.

The three little children breathed a deep sigh of relief, but silently wondered about the safety of those fireproof boots.

Downstairs, the Little Red Christmas Ball was comfortably nestled in his evergreen home. Everything seemed as perfect as a Christmas Eve could be.

Even so, he was on alert for any potential problems among his ornamental colleagues. He knew...he thought...this family depended on him to keep order, and most of all, to set a good example.

"Remember, everyone, shine bright and hold tight," he instructed.

"A branch of my own and a home to cheer. All that a Little Red Christmas Ball could want."

The family now gathered before the crackling fire, reading aloud the familiar tales of Christmas long ago. The Little Red Christmas Ball listened closely to all of his favorites. There were stories of reindeer, and even some ghosts. A story of shepherds and wandering kings; of the star they followed, through the darkness that night.

"My goodness, look at the time!" said the Mommy as the final carol of the night was sung. "We'd all better get to bed because—"

"Tomorrow's a busy day!" sang the others, and Mommy joined in their laughter.

Together they stood and marveled at the beauty of their own special tree. It was wrapped in love and lit up the darkness of their own special night.

A night of wonder. A night of magic. A Christmas night.

An ideal night to be a Little Red Christmas Ball.

Part IV
"Shine Bright and Hold Tight"

"**OK** everybody, let's hit those sacks," said the Daddy in that peculiar language that Daddies sometimes use. "Somebody turn off the Christmas tree lights."

"I will do it, I will do it, Daddy," cried the littlest boy.

"I'm not sure you can reach it," said the Daddy.

"I can, I can reach it, Daddy."

"Ok son, hurry up...but be careful."

"I will Daddy, I will," said the littlest boy as he ran toward the tree.

The Little Red Christmas Ball snapped to attention, for this was when a Little Red Christmas Ball's most important work really began. At night, when the family was asleep, preparing the tree for Santa. Shining bright when there weren't any lights.

The littlest boy anxiously surveyed the tree.

"Hmmmm, now where did Daddy plug in this ol' tree? Oh, there it is, way back there. I bet I can reach that...I think," said the boy.

The littlest boy knelt on the edge of the sofa and reached. Way toward the back he reached. Through some of the branches, he reached and reached and reached for the switch.

The Little Red Christmas Ball watched all this with concern.

Concern for the boy....

"Don't fall off the couch...."

And concern for the tree....

"Careful now...be very careful...."

...Considering what had already occurred....

With all his concerns, the Little Red Christmas Ball hadn't even noticed that in order to reach the switch, the littlest boy had pushed his small evergreen branch all the way towards the back of the tree.

"There's that ol' switch," said the littlest boy as he reached down and clicked off the lights.

"Thank goodness," said the Little Red Christmas Ball, putting his concerns to rest; yet still unaware of his own perilous situation.

"Come on son, up to bed," said the Daddy from the top of the stairs.

"Here I come!" shouted the littlest boy, who then let go of the straining limb.

The little branch abruptly snapped back.

"Whoooa...here we go again!" cried the Little Red Christmas Ball, as he shot forward, then backward. Up and then down.

"Shine bright...hold tight," repeated the Little Red Christmas Ball, over and over again.

But the Little Red Christmas Ball couldn't shine bright enough. Didn't hold tight enough...and suddenly found himself, astonishingly...tumbling, down and across the tree.

Glittering flashes of red bounced from limb to lower limb. The Little Red Christmas Ball tried desperately to hook on to a branch, any branch at all. But his worst fears had come true. He was hookless, and quietly...softly...he fell to the carpet, below.

Behind the stack of presents he rolled and rolled and rolled. To the farthest corner, behind the Christmas tree, he rolled...then gently came to a stop.

Dizzy and confused, the Little Red Christmas Ball slowly opened his eyes. Perhaps this was all a bad dream...he prayed. Perhaps it was only mid-summer and he was still wrapped in his box...he hoped.

But sadly, the Little Red Christmas Ball knew this wasn't a dream at all.

He knew he had fallen from the tree.

He knew Christmas would pass him by.

He knew he could no longer be a Little Red Christmas Ball.

He knew there were tears in his eyes....

Part V
"Rolling, Rolling"

In the quiet dark of this enchanted night, the Little Red Christmas Ball sat waiting...waiting once again. Waiting for his situation to improve.

I can't stay like this all night, he thought. Something will soon happen. It has too. Doesn't it?

Slowly, with each passing minute—seeming like lifetimes to a lost, little Christmas ball—he realized...nothing would happen. His situation would not change...unless, of course, he did something to change it himself. After all, he was a Little Red Christmas Ball and he could shine bright through any night.

The first thing he needed to do was to get out from behind

this stack of presents.

"No one will ever find me back here; and worst, I might be crushed if Santa knocks a box over," shuddered the Little Red Christmas Ball.

So with all the energy of stored hopes and dreams he'd collected through the years, the Little Red Christmas Ball began to shine. Shined so bright, he lit up the room with the glow of his love and determination.

Suddenly, the Little Red Christmas Ball began to vibrate and shake. It seemed as if the little ball would explode from within.

"I am a Little Red Christmas Ball and I will not miss a Christmas.

"I am a Little Red Christmas Ball and I will not miss a Christmas," he said, over and over again.

Then, by the sheer force of his will and strength of his love, the Little Red Christmas Ball actually began to roll. He rolled away from the packages. He rolled towards the center of the tree. And from the center of the tree he was able to roll closer and closer to his little evergreen home.

"I'm doing it, I'm doing it!" cried the Little Red Christmas Ball. "I'm actually rolling! I am a Little Red Christmas Ball and I can do anything, anything at all!"

But sadly, this was not the case, as the Little Red Christmas Ball was soon to find out.

Rolling toward his tiny branch, the Little Red Christmas Ball was overjoyed with all he'd accomplished. It had been quite a feat, quite a feat indeed for a Little Red Christmas Ball. However, as he looked up toward the limb from which he had fallen, his hope and high spirits suddenly fell, as he himself had fallen.

The tiny limb was not as low as he had thought. In fact, from where he sat now, it seemed to be as high as any branch on the tree.

As a Little Red Christmas Ball, of course I can roll. What kind of ball would I be if I couldn't roll, he thought.

"But, I could never raise myself off the ground and on to that branch, not on my own."

Slowly, his warm, shining glow faded as a lifetime of hope and an eternity of dreams trickled away....

Part VI
Cheese & Cookies

Time passed, as time always does, and the Little Red Christmas Ball stared helplessly up toward his forever lost home.

"How could I have been so silly....how could I have been so unhappy to spend the holiday on that perfectly fine, little branch? I would give anything, now, to share even the lowest branch on the back of the tree."

Suddenly, from around the corner came a dark, blurry movement. Actually, it was a dark, grey, furry, blurry movement. Actually, it was a dark, grey, furry, blurry... mouse. Not a singing, unidentifiable mouse, but an actual, real live, house mouse.

"Say...hello there," said the mouse to the Little Red Christmas Ball. "Allow me to introduce myself, I am the House Mouse. And who might you be?"

The Little Red Christmas Ball turned his drooping eyes toward the source of this unwanted disturbance.

"What...what is it, what are you saying...what do you want?" he said in a weary voice.

"I say, I am the House Mouse and you look like someone who's carrying a whole lot of worry on your back....if you had a back, that is."

The Little Red Christmas Ball's spirits rose at the sight of this potential tiny rescuer.

"Why, I am the Little Red Christmas Ball, perhaps you may have noticed—oh, never mind all that," he said, his excitement starting to grow.

Perhaps this fuzzy, little mouse could help him with his trouble. Perhaps this little house mouse could help him get back home.

"You see," continued the Little Red Christmas Ball, "I've fallen from the tree, and if I don't get back in time for Christmas, what kind of Little Red Christmas Ball would I be?"

With great enthusiasm and much attention to detail, the Little Red Christmas Ball told the House Mouse the entire story of his misadventure.

"...and so, you see, being a ball and all, I was able to roll myself to this very spot. But now I must find a way to return to that branch, waaaaaay up there. You see, I must find a way, I must, I must, I must! Do you think you can help? Do you know of a way?"

The House Mouse stood for a moment, deeply lost in thought. Scratching his large mousey ears, he appeared to be pondering this puzzling situation.

The Little Red Christmas Ball brightened with this measure of hope.

"Say, have you seen any cheese?" said the House Mouse to the Little Red Christmas Ball. "I haven't eaten in minutes and I could sure use some cheese."

"What? Cheese...what cheese?" said the Little Red Christmas Ball. "Haven't you listened to a word I've said? I must get back to that limb, waaaaaay up there, and all you can think of is cheese?"

"Well," said the House Mouse, looking waaaaaay up there at the bare evergreen perch. "That is quite a ways. You must have taken quite a tumble. I sure would've liked to have seen that. You see I was looking for some cheese...."

"How can you be thinking of eating at a time like this? If I don't get back on the tree by the time Santa arrives, I will have missed all of Christmas and then there could never be another...at least, not for me"

"I'm sorry," said the House Mouse. "I wish I could help ya out. You see, the fact is, finding cheese and eating it is what I do. I'm just a House Mouse and if there was a way I could help you, I'd be happy to give it a shot. But I could never lift you on my back and carry you up that tree. I wish I could, I really, really do. I also wish I had some cheese right now, but facts is the facts. Know what I'm sayin?"

"Perhaps you have some friends or family nearby that could be of some assistance. Together, I'm sure, we could find a way," said an anxious Little Red Christmas Ball.

"Nope, I'm sorry, once again," said the House Mouse. "I live here all by my lonesome. Good luck all the same. Let me know if you see any cheese. Maybe we could split it... uhm...fifty-fifty. If you like cheese, that is. You don't eat cheese...do ya?"

"Cheese...cheese, of course I don't eat cheese," said the

Little Red Christmas Ball. "In fact I don't eat anything at all. I brighten this home at Christmas time and help spread holiday good cheer. If I don't get back to my little green branch soon, I'll have no purpose...no purpose at all."

"I didn't think so," said the House Mouse pondering the situation a little bit further.

Hmmmm, while I could still use a nice piece of cheese, he thought, I guess it wouldn't hurt to take a minute and try to help this poor Little Red Christmas Ball.

"Let's see now, where exactly is it that you fell from?"

"Waaaay up there," said the Little Red Christmas Ball.

"Ok, ok, ok, I'll tell you what I'm gonna do," said the House Mouse. "You sit tight while I climb up this here tree and peruse the situation. Maybe I'll think of an idea, and besides, there just might be some cheese stuck up there, somewhere."

In the blink of an eye, the House Mouse was again a furry, blurry dot, darting up the Christmas tree.

The Little Red Christmas Ball watched with envy as his fuzzy, new friend scurried from limb to limb.

"Say, there sure are some interesting characters up here," said the House Mouse. "Do you know these guys? A moose and some dancing birds. And some sort of strange creatures singing under a big red cap. Kinda rude too if you ask me, which you haven't of course. None of them seemed especially interested in cheese."

"Will you pleeeease stop with the moose and those penguins and cheese? What do you see, what can you do, have you gotten any ideas?" asked a desperate Little Red Christmas Ball.

"Oh yeah, sorry about that," said the House Mouse, bouncing out to the little green limb. "This really isn't very high after all. If we only had a length of rope or string, maybe, just maybe now, I could hoist ya up. If I had the strength of course. Maybe if I took a little cheese break...."

"String, a rope, hoist me up...yes, yes! That just might work," cried the Little Red Christmas Ball. "String, string... strings the thing. Where could we find some string? We must find some string."

Just then, wandering out from under the woodwork, nibbling on a small crumb of cookie, an odd looking creature with dangling antennae happened upon the Little Red Christmas Ball and House Mouse loudly discussing the priority of a string search versus a cheese search.

"Yipe!" exclaimed the House Mouse, startled by this long legged, winged creature. "Oh, it's just you, Cookie. Why do you always sneak around like that?"

"Why I'm a cock-a-roach, dear boy," replied Cookie Cock-a-Roach. "It is precisely what I do. Sneak around and look for food. Then I disappear in a snap; faster than the speed of light."

"Say, you haven't come across a piece of cheese have ya? I am just about to faint from hunger."

"No...no cheese. Lots of cookies though," said the munching cock-a-roach. "Always plenty of cookies in this house. Why there is one whole cookie I have been working on for over a year. I'd certainly like to find another one of those. Oatmeal, preferably"

"Excuse me for interrupting," said the Little Red Christmas Ball, politely maintaining his patience. "All this talk of cheese and cookies is very interesting, but you see, I am the Little Red Christmas Ball and I've had the terrible misfortune to have fallen from this tree. The House Mouse was kind enough to try and help me return to my branch in time for Christmas and—"

"How very rude of me, indeed, my dear sir. I am the

Cookie Cock-a-Roach, with the hyphenated A. It appears I have been so busy going about my own selfish business that I didn't even notice your dreadful plight. Please, tell me how I might be of assistance."

"Well, we were looking for some cheese," said the House Mouse." You see it's important I maintain my strength throughout this terrible ordeal."

"No, no, no," shouted the Little Red Christmas Ball, his frustration growing with every lost second. "We need to find a length of string or cord. Something we can tie to my loop and lift me to my branch, waaaaay up there."

"Hmmmmm, string, string. Where did I see some string? Why I believe there was some string in the kitchen, behind the stove. There is always all sorts of fascinating materials back there," said Cookie.

"Why that's wonderful, absolutely fantastic!" said the Little Red Christmas Ball. "If you would be so kind as to go and retrieve it, the House Mouse and I—"

"Now, come to think of it, that wasn't a length of string at all," said Cookie Cock-a-Roach. "Silly me, I believe that was an excellent piece of long forgotten spaghetti. Delicious too, if I might add. Why I feasted on that for a week. It's always such a treat to—"

"Say, do you think there might be some cheese back there, Cookie?" said the House Mouse, wiggling his ears in hungry anticipation.

The Little Red Christmas Ball despaired, once more. While it seemed the House Mouse and Cookie Cock-a-Roach were willing to help, they were terribly preoccupied with food. Eating it and talking about it.

Despite his two hungry visitors, he sat alone in his sadness, as the minutes tick...tick ticked away.

The Little Red Christmas Ball had no idea what time it was, but he knew it was getting later and later. Santa would soon be here....

Part VII
"Hopes and Dreams"

The Little Red Christmas Ball quietly listened to the House Mouse and Cookie Cock-a-Roach, with the hyphenated A, debate the nutritional values of cheese and cookies. Suddenly, he felt a soft tap tap, tap tapping. As he slowly turned around he was startled by the sight of a long, silky, black appendage, poking out from within the Christmas tree.

"Excuse me," said a soft, gentle, lady-like voice from among the branches. "I am Spindy Spider and I'm afraid I have been eavesdropping on your conversation. Perhaps I can be of some assistance in your hour of need."

"Oh, thank you very much, Ms. Spider. That's very kind of

you," said an unhappy Little Red Christmas Ball. I'm afraid there's nothing to be done for me now. Time has just about run out for this Little Red Christmas Ball. You see, I can certainly shine bright and I usually hold tight...but I just can't fight time. It just ticks, ticks, ticks away.

"I really can't complain...I suppose. I've had many, many happy days and holiday seasons. A lot more than most, and every one a special memory to treasure. I guess I just always assumed there would be Christmases forever."

Spindy Spider crept out upon the limb to comfort the Little Red Christmas Ball. Her soft, majestic body moved slowly forward, propelled by eight long silken legs.

"Now, now, Little Red Christmas Ball, please, don't give up hope. Time hasn't run out. Time can never run out. It just moves on and is replaced with brand new time," she said. "As long as there is some time, you can still keep trying and still keep believing.

"As long as you keep believing, there will always be hope. Time can never harm us...time can only help us.

"Why, time is what allows us to make our dreams come true. And, after all, what would a Christmas be, without our hopes and dreams?"

The Little Red Christmas Ball was cheered by Spindy Spider's encouraging words. In fact, if you looked closely, you could see his shine begin to glow, anew.

"Yes, yes...you're right, Spindy. There is still time...and there is still hope for this Little Red Christmas Ball. What am I doing wasting valuable minutes feeling sorry for myself when there's work to be done? A branch to be conquered and a home to cheer. We will try, try, try and try again!" shouted the Little Red Christmas Ball, glowing brighter and redder by the second.

"Hey, what's with all the shouting," said the House Mouse. "We can hardly hear ourselves squabbling."

"Well, well, somebody has certainly brightened up around here," said Cookie Cock-a-Roach, surprised at the warmth of the Little Red Christmas Ball's glow.

"There is still hope and there is still time," said the Little Red Christmas Ball. "We must try to find a way. Listen to the wise words of Spindy Spider. Oh, I don't believe everyone has met. Spindy, I would like to introduce you to the House Mouse and Cookie Cock-a-Roach. They've been kind enough to take a minute out of their busy schedules to lend me some assistance."

"How do you do, Mr. Mouse...Mr. Cock-a-Roach. It's a pleasure to make your acquaintance," said the soft spoken spider. "I have often seen you both around and about, but I guess we've never had a mutual interest to bring us together. How nice it is to meet new friends."

"Pleased to meetcha," said the House Mouse to Spindy Spider, inspecting her numerous spindly legs. "I'll betcha you could carry lots of cheese with those leggies. Say, you haven't got any...cheese, that is...tucked away some place, do ya?"

"Oh, don't pay any attention to this single minded little mouse," said Cookie. "How do you do, Madam. I am Cookie Cock-a-Roach, with the hyphenated A, at your service. It is indeed our pleasure to meet someone as majestic as you. And please, call me Cookie."

"Why thank you, Cookie," said Spindy.

"Ok, so now that everyone knows each other, let's get busy," said the Little Red Christmas Ball, now more determined than ever.

"Ah, excuse me Little Red Christmas Ball," said the House Mouse. "I don't meanta spoil all of your enthusiasm, but I think you have forgotten that we are still a bit lacking in the string department. Without string, we are stuck, stuck

stuck."

"Hmmmm, I hate to admit it but I do believe our fuzzy little friend has a point," said Cookie. "This is indeed a cheesy situation."

"Cheese...cheese. Did somebody mention cheese?" asked the House Mouse. "Who's holdin out on me? I knew there was cheese. I could smell it. I could smell it a mile away. Come on, come on, come on."

"No one said anything about cheese," said the Little Red Christmas Ball, his frustration returning. "Cookie, you've been all over this house. Isn't there some place you can think of that might have some string lying around."

"I'm afraid not, dear ball. I have been through this house a thousand times, today alone, and I don't recall any string. However, I do believe I might have an alternative plan."

"Really...what sort of alternative plan?"

"Just give me a minute to round up the required objects, dear ball, and I'll show you. House Mouse, please be so kind as to lend me some assistance."

"Why certainly," said the House Mouse.

And in a flash, Cookie Cock-a-Roach and the House Mouse were off.

"Excuse me, once again," said Spindy Spider. "As I said before, I really do believe I can help you."

"Oh, thank you very much Spindy," said the Little Red Christmas Ball to the spider. "But I believe we may have the situation under control now. I wonder what this new plan is? I'll bet it's something really clever."

"But, Little Red Christmas Ball, if you will only listen for a second," said Spindy, yet her pleas went unheeded as Cookie and the House Mouse quickly returned with two large and cumbersome objects.

"What are those things?" inquired, a confused Little Red Christmas Ball.

"Well, my dear red rounded fellow, all this talk of string reminded me of an empty spool of thread that was nearby. The other object is one of those long forgotten, sand papery board things that seem to be hiding in every obscure nook and cranny, especially under sofa cushions."

"Well that's all well and good Cookie, but how will these things help me get back up on my branch?"

"You see, it all has to do with laws of physics, dear ball. We create a fulcrum with the spool and by transferring our weight—"

"Come on Cookie, skip the mumbo jumbo. What's the plan?" asked the House Mouse.

"Simply this, my dear fellows. We place the board on top of the spool. This will create a sort of see-saw. The Little Red Christmas Ball sits on one end of the board, then, the House Mouse and I will jump down onto the other end and spring him up into the tree, whereby Spindy will catch him with her long arms and place him onto the limb. I ask you, what could be simpler?" said Cookie, excitedly.

"I don't know," said the Little Red Christmas Ball. "It sounds a little far-fetched to me."

"Not at all, dear ball, just you wait and see."

So Cookie set off to execute his incredible plan. He carefully arranged the sand papery, emery board and empty spool, calculating for angles of ascent and thrust—lining everything up scientifically to allow the Little Red Christmas Ball to softly land in the cradling arms of Spindy Spider.

"Ok, Little Red Christmas Ball, you sit right there on the end of the board," instructed Cookie. "House Mouse and I will climb up several branches and jump down onto the other end".

"I don't know about this, Cookie," said a skeptical House Mouse. "Maybe if I had some cheese it would make us heavier and—"

"Come, come now, my fuzzy friend, let's go...up the tree with you."

The Little Red Christmas Ball sat cautiously on the end of the board, still not convinced of the value of this plan. He looked toward Spindy Spider, who sat quietly in her web with a knowing look.

"Now, Spindy, if you would be so kind as to take your position on the target limb, we'll be all set," instructed Cookie.

"Why certainly, Cookie, whatever you say," replied Spindy, slowly making her way along the web and out to the branch.

"Are you ready, Little Red Christmas Ball?" shouted Cookie.

"I guess I'm as ready as I'll ever be," answered the Little Red Christmas Ball as he closed his eyes.

"Here we come!" cried Cookie.

"Anchors away!" yelled the House Mouse.

"Oh no," whispered the Little Red Christmas Ball.

The Little Red Christmas Ball seemed to wait an eternity as his two potential rescuers hurled out into space.

KERTHUMP...! went the sound of Cookie Cock-a-Roach and the House Mouse, landing promptly on their individual rear ends, on either side of the board.

The Little Red Christmas Ball opened his eyes, a bit relieved to see they had badly missed the target.

"How very undignified," said Cookie as he rubbed his sore behind.

"Not to mention a pain in the butt," replied the House Mouse.

Spindy looked down from the tree with an amused grin. "Perhaps I might make a suggestion," she said.

"Now, now, not to worry," said Cookie, "just a case of a much needed practice jump. Come on, House Mouse...let's give it another go, shall we."

"I don't know, Cookie," said the Little Red Christmas Ball, "Maybe we should hear what Spindy has to say."

"Places everybody," cried Cookie confidently. "This plan is foolproof."

"Yeah...but maybe not cock-a-roach proof," muttered the House Mouse.

Again, they all assumed their positions to execute this improbable plan.

"Jumping Jelly Beans!" yelled the pair of would be rescuers as they leapt out into space...this time heading directly for the board.

Again, the Little Red Christmas Ball closed his eyes and held his breath.

"KERTHUD!" went the sound as the two landed squarely on their target.

Surprisingly, the Little Red Christmas Ball felt himself rising off the ground. Yes, actually off the ground...he thought....backwards and a mere half inch in height.

Cookie glumly took it all in and felt a bit foolish with the disappointing results of his foolproof plan.

"I'm sorry, Little Red Christmas Ball. I guess I underestimated the weight ratios and—"

"If that means I shoulda had me a piece of cheese, then I told ya so," said the House Mouse in a huff.

"That's alright, Cookie," said the Little Red Christmas Ball, graciously consoling the cock-a-roach. "It certainly was a creative plan. Maybe we should go back to our original idea and try to find some string"

"Excuse me, Little Red Christmas Ball," said Spindy, returning to her comfy web, "but I really do think I can help you."

"Do you mean to say you know where there's some string?" said an animated Little Red Christmas Ball.

"No, not exactly string," said Spindy. "Perhaps I can explain."

"Please, oh please do," said the Little Red Christmas Ball.

"Yes, please enlighten us, dear lady," said Cookie.

"What I wouldn't do for some cheese," said the House Mouse.

Spindy Spider proceeded to tell her attentive new friends the solution she had in mind.

"You see, I am a spindling spider. I spend my time spindling long silky threads and weaving beautiful new webs. Whenever I see a quiet, lonely spot I think needs cheering, I weave my own special magic. In fact, I've been working on a very special decorative web to add to this lovely Christmas tree."

"I see," said the Little Red Christmas Ball, inspecting the wondrous web Spindy had woven from branch to branch. "That is very beautiful indeed, but how can a spider's web be of any use to me?"

"I think you're missing the lady's point, dear ball," said Cookie. "I believe her lovely talent is just the thing we need."

The House Mouse scratched his puzzled ears and asked, "What are we supposed to do, toss him up into the tree until he sticks in the web? Not me, I barely have the strength to stand. Why If I don't get some cheese—"

The Little Red Christmas Ball brightened.

"I get it," he said. "Spindy Spider can spindle a thread as long as we need to hoist me to the tree. That's it...that will get it done. I'm saved, my Christmas is saved; all is not lost after all. Hooray!" cried the Little Red Christmas Ball.

The House Mouse and Cookie Cock-a-Roach joined hands and triumphantly danced around the Little Red Christmas Ball in joy. Together, they had saved the day...they thought.

"Excuse me, once again," said Spindy to the celebrating trio. "I don't mean to dampen your high spirits.

"That is my plan, it's true. But I do have one fear."

"Fear, fear, what sort of fear?" asked the Little Red Christmas Ball, diminishing a bit.

"I have a fear of starvation," said the House Mouse.

"Please, dear Ms. Spider, what fear do you harbor?" asked

Cookie.

"While it is true I can spindle a thread as long as you need to lift this Little Red Christmas Ball to his limb, I'm afraid my webs are as fragile as they are beautiful. Yes, I may be able to double weave and triple weave...even quadruple my weave. But I have never had a test as great as this."

"Thank you, Spindy, for sharing your concern and doubt with us," said the Little Red Christmas Ball. "However, as I see it, there is no other choice. I'm willing to take the risk. At least I will have tried."

"That's the spirit!" said Cookie, full of cock-a-roach bravado.

"I know we can do it!" said the House Mouse, forgetting his lack of cheese, for once.

"Spindy Spider, please...weave your special magic for me," said a determined Little Red Christmas Ball.

Part VIII
"Weaving the Plan"

The threesome sat mesmerized as Spindy Spider raised her magical spinnerets. From numerous spinning spools, long streams of liquid hardened to form beautiful strands of silken thread. Over and over, Spindy spun the threads to create a weave that would—hopefully—carry the Little Red Christmas Ball back to his longed for perch.

"Wow!" said the House Mouse. "I've never seen anything like this before!"

"It's the most beautiful thing I have ever encountered," said Cookie Cock-a-Roach, clearly entranced.

The Little Red Christmas Ball gazed at Spindy Spider's wizardry and said, "I hope it'll be strong enough...it just has to...I know it will. I'm the luckiest Little Red Christmas Ball, to have such friends as these."

Spindy Spider continued her spinning, wrapping thread over delicate thread, around and around to create a tightly woven weave.

Finally, after much work and intense concentration, Spindy completed her miraculous chore. Now, drained of energy, she laid back in her web.

"I have spun it long and I have spun it strong. It's the best I can do, Little Red Christmas Ball. I hope it is enough."

Coiled before them lay a delicate length of magically entwined cord. Perhaps not strong enough to lift many things, but certainly strong enough to bear the weight of a Little Red Christmas Ball...perhaps.

Part IX
"Flight Into Night"

"Spindy, I don't know what to say or even how to say it," said the Little Red Christmas Ball.

"This is truly a work of art, dear lady," said Cookie as he carefully inspected the line. "A miraculous work of art."

The weary spider lifted her tired, brown eyes and said, "Thank you for your kind words. It was truly my pleasure, but I fear you must now concentrate on the task at hand or all my efforts will have been wasted."

"Yes," said the Little Red Christmas Ball. "I can feel the air beginning to tingle. Santa must be getting closer."

The House Mouse wiggled his super sensitive ears and said, "You're right, I can hear the jingle of sleigh bells off in the distance. Faraway...but gettin closer."

"My goodness, those ears are not only large, but quite effective. I suppose we're all blessed with our own special magic," said Cookie, as his long, delicate antennae reacted to the newly charged electric atmosphere. "I guess the trick is putting it to the proper use."

"Alright, let's begin," said the Little Red Christmas Ball, assuming control of his destiny. "House Mouse, take hold of one end of the rope and climb up to the limb. Cookie, when the House Mouse reaches the limb, you tie the other end around my loop. Then, climb up and help the House Mouse hoist me. It should be as simple as that!"

"Yes, indeed it should," said Cookie. "But often the best laid plans of mice and...Little Red Christmas Balls, not to mention...cock-a-roaches...often go awry, ahem, so to speak."

"Nevertheless, we'll neither succeed nor fail if we don't hurry," said the Little Red Christmas Ball; the sound of distant sleigh bells becoming clearer now to everyone.

"Go House Mouse, you must go now!"

The House Mouse wiggled his ears in fierce determination. Picking up the braided end of rope he began to climb. Not as quickly as before, because of his added burden, but nonetheless resolved to help this Little Red Christmas Ball.

Meanwhile, all the other occupants of the tree had stopped and taken notice of the drama unfolding, on this now early, Christmas morn. The Dancing Penguins had stopped dancing. The Singing Mice or squirrels... whatever they are, had stopped singing. Even the Jogging Moose had taken a breather and put aside his cooltoons. They felt, somehow, they were all in this together. And together, they rooted for this heroic Little Red Christmas Ball.

"Ok, I made it. In my weakened condition and all, I made it," said the persistent little House Mouse.

"That's great," said the Little Red Christmas Ball. "An expert job of climbing, if I've ever seen one. Don't you agree Cookie?"

"Why yes, my dear fellow, I couldn't have performed better myself," responded Cookie with a knowing wink of the eye.

"You guys can save the phony sweet talk and think about helping me get my paws on some well-earned cheese when this is all over," said the house wise mouse with a sly smile.

Spindy Spider giggled at this exchange between new friends as she rested in her nearby web.

"If I could, I would find you a whole case of cheese," said the Little Red Christmas Ball, happily. "Now Cookie, fasten the other end of the rope to the silver loop on my top."

"It would be my pleasure, dear ball," said Cookie.

"Make it tight, as tight as you can."

"I am dear ball, as tight as is Cookie Cock-a-Roachedly possible."

"That's great, Cookie, just wonderful," said the Little Red Christmas Ball, but he anxiously wondered just how tight Cookie Cock-a-Roachedly tight actually was.

"Now, when you are able to hoist me up to the limb it should be an easy job for one of you to re-attach my hook and then...I'm home free."

"Yes, yes, dear ball, we will simply re-attach your hook and then we are all home free," said Cookie as his enthusiasm grew with every new accomplishment. "Just tell us where to find this hook."

"My hook...why my hook is...why...my hook...is...missing," said the Little Red Christmas Ball, suddenly deflated.

"Without my hook, I can never be hung on the tree. Without my hook, our plan is no plan at all."

"Perhaps the House Mouse can see your hook from his vantage point on the limb," said Spindy Spider. "Perhaps it's still on the limb itself."

"Another great idea, Spindy," said the Little Red Christmas Ball. "House Mouse is my hook attached to the branch? Please, please say yes, say yes it is."

"I could certainly say yes, Little Red Christmas Ball, but I'm afraid that's not the case," said a befuddled House Mouse. "Lemme look around a little. I'm sure it couldn't have gone too far."

"No, it couldn't have gone too far at all," said a reassuring Cookie.

"No, not too far at all. Not far at all, I'm sure...I hope," whispered the Little Red Christmas Ball.

"Say there, little fella," said a strange new voice to the House Mouse, as he scurried through the tree.

"Whazzit, whozzit, who said that?" cried the startled mouse.

"Sorry to give you such a fright," said the Jogging Moose.

"But I believe you'll find the hook you're looking for, right over there, under that big clump of tinsel."

Sure enough, embedded in one of the clumps of silvery tinsel—placed there hours ago by the impatient littlest boy— was the Little Red Christmas Ball's gleaming silver hook.

"That's it!" cried the House Mouse. "I've found it! Thanks Moosie, I couldn't have done it with outcha."

"No problem," said the Jogging Moose. "It was the least I could do."

"I got it, I got it," shouted the House Mouse as he scurried back out onto the evergreen limb. "The Jogging Moose pointed it out."

"The Jogging Moose," said the Little Red Christmas Ball in astonishment. "This is truly a magical night."

The jingling bells drew closer and closer; louder and louder.

"Quick, Cookie, climb to the limb and help the House Mouse hoist me up. Quickly, quickly, quickly!"

"With the speed of lightning, I am off, dear ball," said Cookie as he zipped away.

The anxious Little Red Christmas Ball looked toward Spindy Spider who returned a reassuring nod.

"We can only try our best, Little Red Christmas Ball, and sometimes we can make our dreams come true."

"I know, Spindy...I know," said the Little Red Christmas Ball. He glanced up at the imposing branch and the great space that stood between them.

"Shine bright and hold tight.

"Shine bright and hold tight.

"Shine bright and hold tight."

Slowly, the length of silken line began to uncoil as the House Mouse and Cookie Cock-a-Roach began to pull. Suddenly, the slack was no more and the line became taut. Astonishingly, the Little Red Christmas Ball...began to rise.

"I'm moving, I'm moving," whispered the Little Red Christmas Ball.

"It's working, it's working!" he shouted out with glee.

"Keep pulling, keep pulling, faster a little faster...but carefully, please be very, very careful." He was so excited he didn't know what else to say. Up, up, up...up, up he rose.

"That's easy for him to say," grunted the House Mouse.

"I'd like to see him try this on a totally empty stomach."

"Just keep working, my fuzzy good fellow and we will all soon receive our just dessert," puffed Cookie.

"Yeah, that's it, now you're talkin my language, Cookie. Dessert, that's the ticket. What I wouldn't do for a little dessert. Maybe a nice piece of cheese cake. Mmmmmm, I can taste it now."

"Please keep your mind on the task at hand," huffed Cookie. "Watch what you're doing, House Mouse...lookout where you're gooooing!"

The Little Red Christmas Ball tried living up to his words, doing his best to shine bright and hold tight. With each passing pull and tug of the rope he slowly bumped up the tree. As he climbed, closer and closer, to his goal, he found himself worrying, more and more, something might happen. He could hear the House Mouse and Cookie starting to squabble about something...again. Probably food, if he knew those two.

"Please be careful. Please pay attention," he thought out loud.

The Little Red Christmas Ball summoned the courage to peek down to see how far he had traveled. He was surprised he'd actually covered quite a distance...yet still quite a distance remained.

"Remember to believe, Little Red Christmas Ball," said Spindy Spider. She watched, wide eyed, as the Little Red Christmas Ball continued to rise and rise. "Shine bright and hold tight!"

"Shine bright and hold tight," repeated the Little Red Christmas Ball. "I just wish those two would concentrate and work a little faster."

Then, suddenly, to his amazement, the Little Red Christmas Ball did begin to rise more quickly—much more quickly. Perhaps just a little too quickly. Actually, he was now ascending at an alarming rate of speed.

"My gosh, what's gotten into those two. I'm really moving now. Perhaps a little too—"

The Little Red Christmas Ball gasped as the House Mouse and Cookie Cock-a-Roach, holding on to the other end of the rope, dropped from the tree as rapidly as he was rising.

The House Mouse smiled sheepishly as they passed and said "Whoops...."

Up, up, up the Little Red Christmas Ball catapulted through the air.

Down, down, down the House Mouse and Cookie Cock-a-Roach crashed to the floor.

"What now?" sighed the Little Red Christmas Ball.

Horrified, Spindy Spider followed the Little Red Christmas Ball's flight into night. While her vision was limited, she saw that the Little Red Christmas Ball had not only fallen off the tree...again...but spiraled out towards the center of the room.

"Well, this is certainly different," said an exasperated Little Red Christmas Ball, as his flight reached its height and he seemed to hang in mid-air. "Going down...I guess," as the laws of gravity ruled.

Thankfully, the carpet was soft and plush, as the Little Red Christmas Ball landed with a cushioned thump and rolled farther out into the cold empty space.

"Oh dear, talk about out of the kettle and into the fire...." said Cookie with much concern.

The House Mouse was about to say something about kettles but thought better of it.

"QUICKLY," roared Spindy Spider, in a voice so fierce and unlike her past, demure manner, it frightened Cookie and the House Mouse to attention.

"GO TO HIM...NOW! SEE IF HE'S ALL RIGHT. BRING HIM BACK HERE...RIGHT AWAY," ordered the spider, as she swung from web to web, to the outer reaches of the Christmas tree.

"Yyyyyyes, Madam, your wish is always our ccccommand," said Cookie, as he grabbed the House Mouse and ran into the darkness.

Jingle Jingle Jingle, went the bells, drawing closer still...

Part X
"Dizzy and Confused...Again"

The Little Red Christmas Ball sat, dizzy and confused...again. Where was he, what happened? Why was it so dark all of a sudden? Why did he feel so cold and alone?

Slowly, his head cleared and the disappointing memory returned. Off in the distance stood the shadowy silhouette of the majestic Christmas tree. He had come so close, and now, he had fallen so far...so far away...and alone. Is this how it ends for this Little Red Christmas Ball? He wondered.

Suddenly, he heard the sounds of voices...familiar voices...familiar squabbling, drifting through the darkness.

"I told you to watch what you were doing. This is all the fault of that bottomless pit you call a stomach."

"My fault, I wasn't the one who brought up dessert. Why I oughtta...."

"Cookie...House Mouse...here...I'm over here," shouted the Little Red Christmas Ball toward the delightful sounds of squabbling. "Over here!"

Cookie stopped short as his antennae perked and the House Mouse's ears widened and wiggled.

"Can you see him?" said the House Mouse. "I don't see too well, out here in the open darkness. I usually stick closer to the walls."

"There, I see him over there!" cried Cookie. "We're on our way, Little Red Christmas Ball. Hold tight."

"That's how this whole adventure began," replied the Little Red Christmas Ball with a giggle. "I didn't hold quite tight enough!"

Their reunion was happy, yet brief, as the sound of distant bells grew louder still. Cookie quickly checked for damage but found, to his relief, the Little Red Christmas Ball was in fine shape. Together, the House Mouse and Cookie rolled the Little Red Christmas Ball back toward the tree, dragging the tattered silken line behind, its tight weave, now unraveling.

"I am pleased to announce our journey was a success and the Little Red Christmas Ball is none the worse for wear!" exclaimed Cookie.

"Oh, I am so pleased," replied Spindy Spider, her soft, gentle manner, returned. "But I'm afraid I cannot say the same for my fine silken weave. It has frayed a bit, as you can see."

"Perhaps a bit, madam, but surely not enough to weaken the whole," said Cookie.

The jingle jingle jingle was right on top of them now and they all looked upward.

"Little Red Christmas Ball, I know the remaining time is short, but I can quickly weave some more magic for you, please let me try," said Spindy.

"No," said the Little Red Christmas Ball. "You've done enough for me, tonight...really...and besides, you've just about exhausted your supply of spinning spools, already. No, the time is now or never.

"If it is meant to be, that I should rest upon this tree, then the twine you have spun, will certainly not become undone."

"Hey, he's a poet and don't know it!" shouted the House

Mouse as he playfully nudged Cookie in the side.

Once again, they all laughed and set out to try again, where they had failed once before.

Jingle jingle jingle jingle jingle....

Part XI
"Now or Never"

Carefully and methodically, they retraced the familiar steps of their rescue plan. The previous failure only made them more determined. Cookie decided it was better to learn from their mistake. In fact, he was inspired by it.

"I believe we can improve upon our method of lift," he said. "Actually, I think it is a rather brilliant idea, if I do have to say so myself."

"Never mind the back patting," said the House Mouse. "What's this big idea of yours?"

"Yes, Cookie, please," said the Little Red Christmas Ball. "We have to hurry."

"Ahem...yes as I was saying—"

Softly, Spindy Spider spoke, "I think if Cookie and the House Mouse run the line over your branch and take a position below it, they will be able to create a pulley, which will enable them to lift you more easily."

Cookie appeared a little deflated, "Uhm, yes indeed, that is...uhm, well sort of...basically...I was more or less thinking along the lines of—"

"Cookie, that's a brilliant idea," said the Little Red Christmas Ball. "Quickly, let's get started."

So with great enthusiasm, the House Mouse re-climbed the tree and Cookie re-tightened the cord to the Little Red Christmas Ball's silver loop.

Spindy slowly retreated to her web, trying not to think about the unraveling thread and the magical jing jing jingle of the approaching sleigh bells. She knew, while time was a friend, it did always move on. It was up to us to keep pace with its inevitable flow.

"Ok, ok, ok. I'm all set up, here," said the House Mouse.

Filled with hopeful uncertainty, the Little Red Christmas Ball swallowed hard and said, "Alright, House Mouse, we're just about ready down here too. I just want you to know that

I'll always remember what you've done for me. I know I've taken you away from your cheese and all...."

"Please, Little Red Christmas Ball, don't worry about cheese," interrupted the House Mouse. "There will always be more cheese. I can't think of anything else I'd rather be doing tonight than helping a Little Red Christmas Ball find his way back home."

"Why, my dear little House Mouse," said Cookie Cock-a-Roach, wiping a small tear from his eye. "I see, indeed, we have all come a long way on this magical evening."

"Ah come on, Cookie, don't go gettin mushy on us, now," wisecracked the House Mouse. "Get those skinny little legs of yours up here. We got us a job to do and those jingle bells are jingling right on top of us now."

"Yes sir, one Cookie Cock-a-Roach, coming right up." replied Cookie as he whisked up the tree.

The Little Red Christmas Ball knew the House Mouse was correct. Santa's silver bells were, indeed, directly over the house. Soon they'd hear the soft gentle thud of his sleigh as it touched down on the roof. Then the wondrous sound of his deep belly laugh would follow, rolling down the chimney.

It really was...now or never...for this Little Red Christmas

Ball.

As he gazed toward Spindy, nervously pacing the length of her web, The Little Red Christmas Ball hoped for another encouraging sign. Instead, he saw only her furrowed look of concern.

Undeterred, he looked back towards Cookie and the House Mouse, this time securely in place. He spoke with confidence, "I'm ready when you are. Let's deck these halls!"

"Fa la la la la, la la la............la," sang the Singing Mice or squirrels...whatever they are, as the whole tree came to life with the renewed magic filling the room.

Santa was very, very close.

"One, two, three...pull," said the House Mouse as the two started to tug the fraying thread.

"Steady now, steady," said Cookie as the Little Red Christmas Ball slowly began to rise.

The Little Red Christmas Ball glanced up at the fragile twine. While his progress was certainly smoother than before, he feared the added friction of the threads, rubbing on the branch, would test it even further. However, he knew there was nothing to be done but to shine bright and hold tight.

It was now just a question of who would hold out longer, Cookie and the House Mouse...or the thread.

"We're doing it dear ball, we are doing it," said Cookie as the Little Red Christmas Ball now dangled just below.

"Yeah, just keep shining bright and holding tight," said the House Mouse. "We'll have you hanging in no time, no time at all. And from the sound of that thump on the roof I think we are just in the...St. Nick of time."

The Little Red Christmas Ball nervously giggled, being a bit of a punster himself, and started to think, yes the worst was over. He could smell the fresh scent of evergreen pine embracing him. It had been quite a struggle but now it was all behind him.

Plink...! Plunk...! Plink plunk plink!

Inescapably, one by one, the strands of silken thread began to snap and unravel. Around and around they unwrapped. And around and around the Little Red Christmas Ball spun... around and around and around.

"Oooooooh, here we go again!" he cried. "Cookie...House Mouse...hurry pull...pull as fast as you can."

"Hold on, hold on," shouted Cookie. "Quickly House Mouse, we must work faster. The line is unraveling!"

And pull they did. As fast as a House Mouse and Cookie Cock-a-Roach could. In fact, the Little Red Christmas Ball was so close to home, he could feel the prick of needles as they brushed his face. Spindy Spider swung to the branch and desperately tried to attach the hook to the wildly spinning loop. She had almost grabbed it. It was almost done. He was almost there....

Which made it all the more bitter, when they heard the snap.

Part XII
"A Night of Falls"

The simple, single snap thundered through the hushed little room. The Little Red Christmas Ball was falling. Falling again, in a night of falls. Falling, over and over and over again.

Off the branches he bounced...as he had before.
On the soft cushioned carpet, he landed...as he had before... and he spun and he spun and he spun, like a top...which he hadn't before.

Spindy Spider uselessly stretched her long spindly arm out into the stillness. Cookie Cock-a-Roach and the House Mouse stood quiet and helpless, unlikely twins wrapped in a soft cocoon of unraveled threads. They had failed the Little

Red Christmas Ball, and they felt as lost and as broken as last year's Christmas toys.

On the floor below the Little Red Christmas Ball reeled from his latest fall. He'd gotten pretty used to the landings...by now...but the spinning added a whole new dizzying dimension. He saw, not one pretty Christmas tree, but several; all whirling in a marvelous kaleidoscopic illusion.

He found it kind of enjoyable, actually, and was a little bit disappointed when the effect began to wear off.

He sat alone in the corner, contentedly enjoying the last of the spectacle, when he was joined by a disheartened and concerned Spindy, Cookie, and the House Mouse.

"The poor little fellow seems to be in a state of delirium," said Cookie.

"Is there anything we can do?" asked the House Mouse.

"I'm afraid not," said Spindy. "I'm afraid our time has finally moved on."

And indeed, Spindy Spider was correct. The slumbering night was awakening with the tingle of electric wonder. So much so, that the tiny Christmas tree lights had begun to flicker and the other ornaments had begun to stir. The magic that was Santa was on its way.

Christmas was about to pass the Little Red Christmas Ball by.

Perhaps....

Part XIII
"The Sting of Disappointment and Farewell"

The Little Red Christmas Ball grew aware of the warm, loving presence filling the room. The soft, caressing breeze of giving and forgiveness was as familiar as every past Christmas memory. He saw the shadowed faces of his three caring friends and he slowly began to recall their heroic efforts.

"Thank you...thank you for all you've done for me," said the Little Red Christmas Ball, surprisingly calm and content.

"But Little Red Christmas Ball, we letcha down when you needed to go up...up, up," said the House Mouse.

"Yes, dear ball, how can you possibly thank us for making

such a mess of everything?" asked Cookie. "If only we had more time I'm sure we—"

"No, no." replied the Little Red Christmas Ball. "We had all the time we needed and we gave it our best. That's all we can ever really ask for. Right Spindy?"

Spindy wiped tears from her eyes and replied, "Yes, Little Red Christmas Ball, that's true. Yet, the sting of disappointment is still a heavy weight to bear."

"But the weight I carry is lightened, Spindy, by the new memories I have of the three of you, tonight."

"What's gonna happen now," said the House Mouse, his large fuzzy ears fidgeting.

"Yes, what will become of you, now, dear ball," said Cookie. "Surely someone will find you in the morning and restore you to your rightful place."

"Oh, I don't think I'll be terribly missed, especially this morning. Little Red Christmas Balls don't seem to impress too many people these days. I'll just stay back here, out of sight. Santa will come and unload his presents and inspect the tree, same as he does every year. The newer ornaments will more than make up for my absence. Besides, maybe it's time they got along without me, anyway. I can't keep babysitting these fellows, forever," said the Little Red Christmas Ball, concealing his broken heart. "Besides, I'll be lucky if I'm not crushed under a load of presents."

He chuckled but worried if that was indeed a possibility.

Spindy wrapped her long arms around the Little Red Christmas Ball and hugged him spiderly. "I just wish there was something," she whispered.

Cookie and the House Mouse sadly nodded in agreement.

"Really," said the Little Red Christmas Ball, the hint of a tear starting to form, "you've all given me more than I could ever dream".

The House Mouse clapped his tiny cheeseless paws together and encouragingly said, "I know! We'll all stay right here tonight and have ourselves a real special blow-out Christmas bash. Whadda ya say?"

"No...thank you anyway, House Mouse, but I think now I would just kind of like to be alone for a while...if that's ok."

The others understood and said their sad farewells to the Little Red Christmas Ball and to each other. One by one, they reluctantly disappeared into the lonely dark corners of the awakening house.

Part XIV
"Arrival"

Alone now, the Little Red Christmas Ball sat in the farthest corner behind the tree.

The cozy room absolutely sparkled from the magnificent starlight flowing out from the chimney. Deep from within this magical light came a distant, musical chuckle. Growing louder, it was more like a bellow. But even louder, it rolled like an earthquake. A belly laugh, so deep and so rich it seemed to come from everywhere at once.

Immediately, the Christmas tree was alight with the untapped energy of this awesome night. All of the ornaments began their well-rehearsed routines. The Jogging Moose sprinted for the finish line. The Dancing Penguins danced like it was going out of style, and up above, the Singing Mice or squirrels...whatever they are, let out a blaring chorus of fa la la la la, la la la..........LA!

The Little Red Christmas Ball sat quietly, enraptured by these wondrous events. While he had participated so many times before, he'd always been so concerned with his own special task of shining so red and shining so bright, that he had never appreciated the majesty of it all.

His troubles were miles behind him, now, his mind empty of all thoughts; all except the magic that was before him.

From out of the glittering light stepped the figure of a small, rounded man with a brilliant white beard. It was as blinding as a blizzard wind. He was dressed, of course, in a familiar red suit, trimmed with soft, white fur...and shining, black boots, now forever fire proofed, in the minds of some.

"HO! HO! HO!" bellowed the man as he hitched up his belt and picked up his sack full of surprises. "If I've said it once, I've said it...quite a few times tonight, I would imagine. No real way of knowing the exact number of course, unless I start keeping a count, but I don't suppose too many are actually interested, and I think Santa is just a little too busy tonight, of all nights, to begin counting ho ho ho's. Besides, it's expected, I suppose. Not that anyone ever hears me. Oh no, Santa is much too quick for that. Drives the missus crazy, though. Ho ho this and ho ho that," he said to himself with a small chuckle.

"Guess I shouldn't talk to myself, too much. Folks might get the wrong idea if I were to wake up all the little kiddies. Just gets to be a little monotonous, all this roof hopping, after so many years."

Santa inspected his surroundings and immediately knew this was a familiar house, full of love and warmth.

"Yes, yes I do remember this cozy little home. Lots of goodness under this roof, lots of good indeed.

"Well, what's this now, a plate full of cookies and a nice glass of milk. Let's see that would be...who knows how many helpings of cookies and milk I've had tonight. What I wouldn't give for a nice sandwich and an ice cold...but then, what would the missus say? And this old suit is getting just a tad too tight in the seat, I suppose. HO!HO!HO!" bellowed the jolly old man. "Oops, there I go again with the ho ho hos."

Santa Claus plopped himself down on the soft sofa pillows and propped his weary feet up on the foot rest. He sampled an assortment of cookies and pocketed the rest for the road. After all, he still had a long night ahead.

"Better not forget these carrots for the team. No wonder they always insist on stopping here first, in this part of the world. Not too many folk think about the reindeer's supper. After all, they do most of the heavy work. HO!HO!HO!" bellowed the round little gentleman, patting his ample belly.

"Get it...heavy, I said heavy...work, HO!HO!HO! ...uhmmmm, well I guess it wasn't all that funny," he said, looking about self-consciously. "It's a wonder I don't drive the missus completely out of her mind, HO!HO.....ahem, yes now, um, where was I, now," said the eccentric old man, catching himself in mid-ho.

The Little Red Christmas Ball peered through the branches, chuckling at this wonderful old man. Santa was so full of love and dedication that he was hardly aware of his own special place in our hearts. He seemed to be in particularly good spirits tonight, although, wasn't he always, thought the Little Red Christmas Ball.

Sitting back with his feet propped up, finishing the last of his milk, Santa marveled at the wonder of this beautiful Christmas tree.

"My, oh my. I remember all the splendid trees that have adorned this home, year after year. They've always been decorated with a special love and care. I just don't know what it is, this year...something special. Oh well, there's plenty of work, still to be done, tonight," said Santa as he rose to his feet and approached the tall tree, absently stroking his beard.

"Something special...indeed."

Part XV
"Something Special"

Santa began to go about his happy business of

filling the large Christmas stockings with all sorts of goodies.

"Ho! These seem to get a little bit bigger every year, now don't they?"

And the larger task of unloading his enchanted sack full of presents. As he knelt closer to the tree he chuckled at the spectacle of all the performing ornaments.

Still, Santa was a bit puzzled by something.

"Something special about this tree...." he pondered.

One by one, Santa placed items under the tree.

One by one the Little Red Christmas Ball felt enclosed by the walls of fate.

"At least Santa is careful. He won't let them tumble down on me...." he hoped.

Finishing his task, Santa nimbly hopped to his feet and prepared to leave this cheerful home. Still, something continued to bother him as he stroked his long white whiskers.

"Something, something, something...special," he muttered to himself.

Behind the wall of presents, the Little Red Christmas Ball slowly closed his eyes, beginning his long, long hibernation ...perhaps, this time, forever. Santa was leaving now, and at last, Christmas had indeed passed him by.

He was a Little Red Christmas Ball and his life was to shine bright and help spread Christmas cheer. Now, he had no purpose, and his shine had just about run out. Still...he had his memories and, of course, he would always cherish the special friendships he had made tonight. That would soften his slumber and ensure it was a pleasant one....

The Little Red Christmas Ball quietly let out a yawn and he... slowly...drifted...off....

"HO HO HO HO HO!" bellowed Santa, as his jolly, round face loomed large thru the branches and startled the Little Red Christmas Ball awake.

"Something special! Something very special...is missing from this Christmas tree. I knew it right away," shouted the magical old man.

"Santa!" exclaimed the astonished Little Red Christmas Ball.

"My, my, my, this is somewhat of a predicament you've gotten yourself into, Little Red Christmas Ball," said Santa. "What are you doing way back there, all by yourself, little fellow?"

The Little Red Christmas Ball stared in amazement at the soft gentle face, freshly aglow with rosy red cheeks from the night chill. He felt incapable of speech and began to sputter.

"Uh uh uh uhm...well...uhm...Santa...it seems—is it really you...Santa? It seems...I was shining bright but...I'm afraid to say...not quite holding tight, and I fell from my branch waaaaay up there. Well, actually, just a little below your chin...right there."

"I see," said Santa, sympathetically. "And you've been sitting here alone in the dark, all this time, waiting for this great wonderful Christmas to pass you by?"

"No, no Santa, not at all," replied the excited Little Red Christmas Ball.

He never imagined he would ever actually talk with Santa Claus. Not even in his dreams. He always thought Santa didn't have time for simple Little Red Christmas Balls.

"You see, my friends the House Mouse, Cookie Cock-a-Roach and Spindy Spider were kind enough to help me devise a—"

"Hi ya, Santa," said the House Mouse as Cookie, Spindy and he slowly emerged from the shadows.

"Well now, what do we have here?" said Santa, amused by the sight of these three little rescuers. "I can see you folks have certainly put in a hard nights work."

Santa picked up and inspected the fragile little line that had unraveled into a thousand separate strands.

"My, oh my, who's responsible for this beautiful piece of work," he said, noticing the intricate webbing Spindy had spun throughout the tree.

"Why I am, Santa," said Spindy, softly, as she climbed up to her web. "I created it in honor of your arrival tonight."

"Why thank you, Spindy," said the jolly, little man, clearly touched by this beautiful work of art...and love. "But the real gift you three provided, this night, is to have given this Little Red Christmas Ball hope and most of all...friendship."

"But my dear, Santa," said Cookie clearly confused by this kind man's generosity, "I am afraid we have failed the poor boy. All we were able to provide him with is a few more bumps and bruises."

"Well now...is that how you see it, Little Red Christmas Ball?" asked Santa.

"No...not at all," said the Little Red Christmas Ball. "Why without their help and encouragement, I would have given up long ago. I would never have felt the companionship of true friends...and most of all...I would never have had so much fun. These three have made all the difference."

"That's right," said Santa. "And old Santa never misses a good deed from the heart. Let's see what we have in here."

Santa fumbled through his sack of goodies.

"I believe I have a pretty fair size piece of... cheese...right here."

The House Mouse shook his head and wiggled his fuzzy ears at the sound of the magic word.

"Genuine Swiss, I believe...from a pretty little house in the

Alps. Somehow I thought it might come in handy, tonight. Can I interest anybody in some cheese?"

Santa gently placed the huge hunk of cheese in front of a wide eyed House Mouse.

"I've never seen so much cheese. It's even bigger than me!"

The others laughed heartily as the delighted little mouse crawled in and out of the numerous genuine Swiss cheese holes, not knowing where to begin.

"And for you, my good fellow," said Santa, as he pulled a large oatmeal cookie from the bag and placed it in front of Cookie Cock-a-Roach, "precisely made to your specifications, I believe."

"I am truly undeserving, sir," replied Cookie, gratefully.

"And for you, madam," said Santa to the gentle Spindy Spider, "a brand new set of spinning spools, to assist you as you weave your special magic."

"Why thank you, Santa," said Spindy, with surprise. "I'm afraid I did exhaust my supply tonight. How did you ever know it would be just the thing I needed?"

Santa let out a huge belly laugh, and said, "I suppose, little Spindy...that's my special magic."

Santa now turned his attention back to the Little Red Christmas Ball who was shining softly with a glow of delight for his happy new friends.

Gently, Santa reached down, picked up the Little Red Christmas Ball and carried him out from behind the tree.

"Well, now Little Red Christmas Ball, I think we can find a better place for you to spend the holidays, than behind this pile of presents."

"Yes, Santa, that would be wonderful. If you would be so kind as to place me back on that little bare limb, right over there...."

"HO HO HO," bellowed Santa, "I think we can do a little bit better than that, Little Red Christmas Ball."

Santa took hold of the elusive, silver hook and securely attached it to the Little Red Christmas Ball's loop. Standing directly in front of the colorful tree, he reached waaaaay up to the highest branches and placed the Little Red Christmas Ball on a limb that extended directly below the peak of a majestic golden star.

"But Santa," said the Little Red Christmas Ball, his shimmering red patina growing brighter with pride. "This is the most prominent part of the whole Christmas tree. I would never—"

"Yes, Little Red Christmas Ball. What more deserving place is there for one such as you who has always unselfishly shone bright and brought good Christmas cheer and love to so many, for so long?"

"But Santa, all these years, shining bright and reflecting love was as effortless to me as giving is to you. I'm a Little Red Christmas Ball and I only do what I was meant to do. In fact, until tonight, I thought I was hardly even noticed, least of all by you."

Santa smiled and said, "Yes, I'm sorry Little Red Christmas Ball, but it's true; on Christmas Eve, of all nights, my time is very sparse...indeed. I'm afraid I don't always have an opportunity to show my appreciation to all that make this night so memorable, for everyone. Not even the truly remarkable ones like you, Little Red Christmas Ball."

"But, Santa—" said the Little Red Christmas Ball, his shine glowing redder and brighter still.

Santa continued, "Without your remarkable, red shine and glow full of love, this tree would be nothing more than a meaningless decoration. It's you, Little Red Christmas Ball that makes it a magical symbol of hope and dreams. All that is good in the world reflects from you."

The Little Red Christmas Ball shined as bright as the brightest star, in the Northern sky. His friends, the House Mouse, Cookie Cock-a-Roach, with the hyphenated A, and Spindy Spider sat close by on an adjacent limb. They too were shining. Shining with pride and love for this Little Red Christmas Ball.

Santa stepped back into the starlight that flowed from the Chimney.

"I really must be on my way now," he said. "I foresee many, many more happy Christmases for you, Little Red Christmas Ball. Many more generations to touch...and many more homes to cheer. Remember...always shine bright...and please...hold tight.... HO HO HO!"

Then, like stardust in a breeze, the jolly old man disappeared.

Part XVI
"Discovery"

Outside, the first wandering light of dawn crept over the horizon; the mysterious jingle of sleigh-bells fading as Santa and his reindeer flew into the western sky, chasing the elusive night.

Inside, the room was awash with the loving glow of the Little Red Christmas Ball. High on the tree, he had never felt so complete, so meaningful.

From the stairway came the sneaky sound of several pairs of tiny feet. Carefully peeking around the edge of the doorway, three sets of eyes opened wide as the littlest boy cried out with surprise, "SANTA'S BEEN HERE!"

Behind them, trudging slowly down the stairs, came the Mommy and the Daddy wiping sleep from their pre-dawn eyes.

"Look at the stockings!" cried the little girl.

"Look at the cookies, they're all gone!" gasped the older little boy.

"Look at the tree...it's all lit up, brighter than ever!" said the littlest boy.

The Mommy and the Daddy looked at the Christmas tree...looked at their children...and looked at each other.

"Son," said the Daddy to the littlest boy, "I thought you turned off the lights last night."

"I did Daddy, honest I did. Look the switch is off."

Retreating further back into the tree, the House Mouse, Cookie and Spindy, silently giggled at all the confusion. They had never enjoyed such a Christmas before.

"Hmmmmm..." said the Daddy, inspecting the switch. "It must be some kind of a short or something."

"Daddy...Mommy, look! It's the Little Red Christmas Ball!" said the littlest boy, his eyes full of wonder. "Look how high he is!"

"Look how shiny he is," said the little girl.

"Look how red he is," said the older little boy.

The littlest boy stood on the highest edge of the sofa, and reached as far up as he could reach and said, "Feel how warm he is."

The Daddy turned to the Mommy and asked, "Did you...?"

"Not me...." said the Mommy.

The Daddy then stepped closer to the tree and gently touched the Little Red Christmas Ball. Feeling the warmth of love, he suddenly filled with memories of the little boy he had once been, and of all the past Christmases this special Little Red Christmas Ball had brightened for him. In the deep red reflection, he re-discovered the sparkle that once again shined in his very own eyes.

The Jogging Moose jogged. The Dancing Penguins danced. The Singing Mice or squirrels, whatever they are, sang...Fa la la la la, la la la.........LA!

Oh, and of course...it was snowing....

97

Brian Moloney

Acknowledgements

Special thanks to early readers of The Little Red Christmas Ball — Betsy, Jim, Tom, Wendy, Kat, Joanne, Shannon and Courtney—for their encouragement, critiques and direction, along the way. Lastly, but not leastly, much appreciation to Pami for dotting my I's, crossing my T's and minding all my P's and Q's...which have been known to get unruly, from time to time.

About the Author

Brian Moloney (that's me) has worked in the communications fields of Advertising, Film and TV on both the commercial and corporate sides, since 1978. He (still me) began freelancing as a writer in 1992, when he discovered he could type on a computer without the need of whiteout to hide all his mistakes; a process he found extremely messy and time consuming. In addition to "The Little Red Christmas Ball", he's authored "The Kingdom of Keys", a Young Adult, Action/Adventure/Fantasy story, available thru all major on-line booksellers. Currently, he's at work compiling a collection of essays from his on-line, humor column "The Freelance Retort", which he threatens to finish and send out soon...very, very soon.

"The Freelance Retort" can be found on-line at
http://freelanceretort.blogspot.com/
And on Facebook, along with all the cats and everything else....
Email the Author: freelanceretort@gmail.com

Also Available thru Major On-line Booksellers

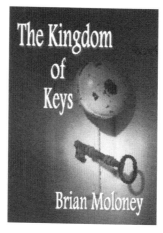

Sixteen year old Toby Pierce is lost, disillusioned and just not happy with the path his life has taken ever since circumstances, four years earlier, changed the course of *everything* he knew as normal. That is, until he discovered the key...*always the key*...to the mysterious *Door to Nowhere*, a perpetually locked, never used, sealed doorway, tucked in the corner of his room.

A strange prophetic dream leads Toby to confront the key and - with the semi-unflagging support of his two best friends, Lori and Billy—unlock the *Door to Nowhere*. An explosive reception soon follows as the trio is transported to the magical *Kingdom of Keys*, where Toby chooses to follow the path of the *Doors*. There, he struggles to learn the secret of the seed...the heart...the soul...the passion...the mind...and most of all, how really simple it all is...if we just have the faith to *allow it to be*....

Action, adventure, fantasy, humor, villains, heroes, Kings, Queens, strange creatures from an enchanted land and a multitude of laser blasts; these are the fundamental elements of *The Kingdom of Keys*. But, more importantly, woven within is an insightful message designed to encourage young minds to choose the path in life most in harmony with, not only their intellect, but also their heart and their soul.

Made in the USA
Charleston, SC
04 October 2016